D1107887

The Happy Lion in Africa

by Louise Fatio   pictures b

McGRAW-HILL BOOK COMPA

THE HAPPY LION
N AFRICA

oger *Duvoisin*

YORK TORONTO LONDON

Also by Louise Fatio and illustrated by Roger Duvoisin

THE HAPPY LION

THE HAPPY LION AND THE BEAR

THE HAPPY LION ROARS

THE THREE HAPPY LIONS

THE HAPPY LION'S QUEST

LE BON LION

LE BON LION EN AFRIQUE

LES TROIS BONS LIONS

A DOLL FOR MARIE

RED BANTAM

Library of Congress Catalog Card Number: 55-8896

SEVENTH PRINTING

Printed in the United States of America.

Monsieur Flambeau traveled all over France with his circus.
But wherever he went,
the clowns and the acrobats did their tricks for empty seats,
and there was no one to applaud when the seal played the trumpet.
"Ah, *là là!*" lamented Monsieur Flambeau one day
when his circus had stopped in a lovely old town.
"If I only had the Happy Lion from the town zoo,
this famous Happy Lion everyone loves
and everyone goes to see in his house in the park,
THEN THERE WOULD BE NO EMPTY SEATS!"

And that is why Monsieur Flambeau kidnaped the Happy Lion.
One moonless night, he entered the park with a lion cage.
"Petit, petit, petit," he called in his gentlest voice,
after opening the door of the lion house.
The Happy Lion, who was always glad to see a friend,
jumped into the cage, and that was that.

The next day the whole town was very sad.
People talked of the news on every street corner.
"Quelle horreur," they said, "our Happy Lion has left us."

In the Happy Lion's garden,
François, the keeper's son, sat on a rock and cried.
"My beloved Happy Lion, where, where has he gone?"

"Where is that man taking me?" moaned the Happy Lion.
"To think that I took him for a friend!"

Monsieur Flambeau drove on until he came to a harbor
where big ships stood with their smokestacks smoking.
Just as the cage came to a stop, the door jolted open.
The Happy Lion jumped out
and went to hide in the first hole he saw.
It was a hole darker than the night.
It was the hold of a ship!

Crouched behind a crate, the Happy Lion
was soon quite frightened by the big ship noises
which began to fill the hold—
noises of chains and steel doors, of bells and machines.
The ship had started on its way!

It rolled for days on high seas.
And the lion was so gloomy behind his crate in the black hold—
so hungry too.
"I so wish to know where I am and where I am going," he sighed.
He did not dare to come out.
What if Monsieur Flambeau was also in the hold?

But at last the ship anchored in a small port of Africa.
As soon as the hatch opened,
the Happy Lion ran out into the sunlight.
He ran all across the busy town,
he ran until he entered the dark forest.

Now it was all very well to be safe from Monsieur Flambeau,
but night brought out the beasts of the forest,
that croaked, and moaned, and screeched,
and wailed, and howled, and snarled.
The lion was frightened all over again
and made himself small at the foot of a tree.
"How far I must be from my beautiful park," he sighed,
"my cool park where the cricket and the nightingale
sing their lovely songs.
And my dear François, how worried he must be!"
The lion wandered a long time in the forest.
It was so hot and humid, like the inside of a kettle.
He ate nothing but bugs and caterpillars,
and dreamed of the steaks that once were his daily fare.

One day, at the edge of a plain, he almost jumped for joy
when he saw a herd of zebras drinking at the water hole.
"They look like Fernand, the zebra at the zoo,
who pulls cartfuls of children on Sundays," he said.
"Surely they will tell me where to eat

and how to find my way home."
But the zebras ran off in a cloud of dust
when they saw the hungry lion.
And the lion went on sadly in the hot sun,
so tired, so hungry, so thirsty, so lonely.

Farther out in the plain, he stopped with a lifted paw
at the sight of giraffes in a clump of trees.
"Who ever saw beasts so tall?" he said with a worried air,
for there were no giraffes in his home zoo.
"Such tall legs and such tall necks.
I must beware of beasts I do not know.
These may be fierce. I must run away."
The giraffes knew a lion when they saw one!
While the lion ran one way, they ran the other way!

In his flight the lion bumped into a rhinoceros
who was asleep in the plain.
"Pardon me," he said. "I am sorry to wake you up."
But the rhinoceros did not see things that way,
and charged the lion with his horn forward.

The lion had barely time to hide behind a tree.
The nearsighted rhinoceros took the tree for the lion
and thrust his horn into it.
He was held like a mouse in a trap.
"Truly," said the lion, walking away,
"this is not a country for a lion."

He wandered about here and there for some time,
then he went to rest behind some rocks
to forget his hunger in sleep.

It was dawn when an earthquake noise woke him up.
"Elephants," he shouted, "elephants like Toby at the zoo,
who takes peanuts from children's hands!"
"Yohooooo, yohoooooo . . ." he called out.
But those elephants must not have liked lions.
They turned to charge,
and they were like a mountain avalanche.

Happily, there were the rocks. The lion hid under the biggest one
until the elephants forgot about him.
"I will find no friend in this country," sighed the lion.
"When beasts do not run from me, they run after me.
Will I ever see again my white house
where every day my dinner was served—
where the sparrows brought the news from town,
and François visited me after school?"

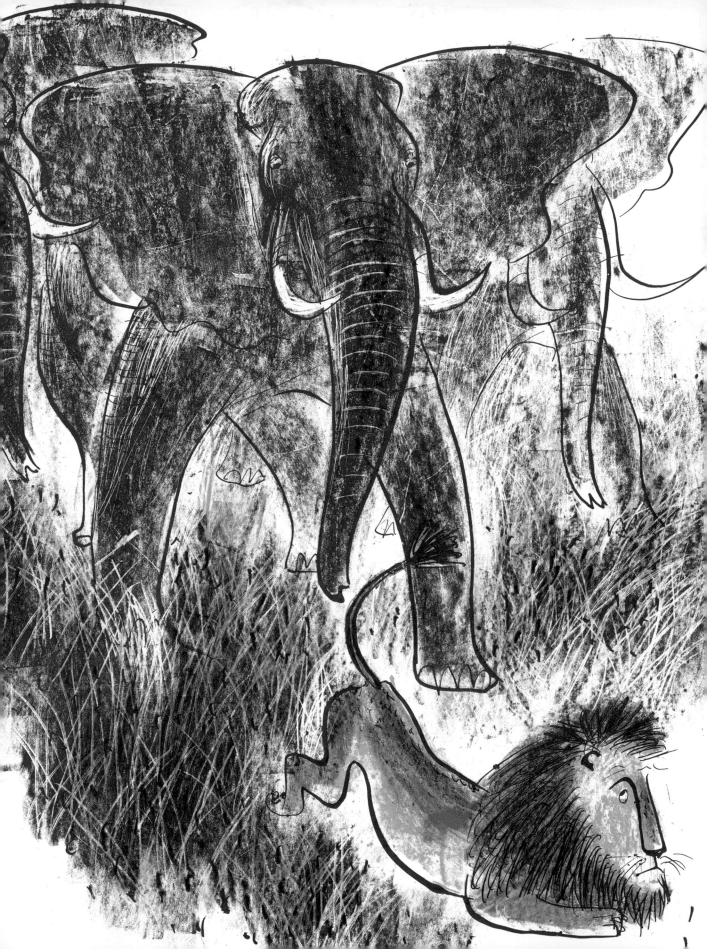

This is how the lion was grieving
when he heard, far away in the plain,
the galloping noise of a herd of antelopes.
They were coming his way.
He could see their sharp horns over the grasses.
"I have had enough of horns," he said, remembering the rhinoceros.
"I must get out of their way."

But antelopes run faster than tired lions,
so he crouched in the grass to let the antelopes go by.
When he looked up again, he could not believe what he saw.
Two lions, just like him, were running behind the antelopes.
He called after them, but they were already too far away.
Sadly, he resumed his lonesome journey
through the tall grass, under the sizzling sun.

He was almost at the end of his strength
when he saw ahead a camp of tents and trucks.
"Men," he roared. "Men, friends, and food."
He crawled to the camp, for he could hardly walk.

He found it empty, but there was a large pan cooking on the fire,
full of great chunks of meat
floating in a well-spiced sauce.
He emptied the pan with a few strokes of his tongue.
Then, well contented, he fell asleep on a cot.

When Monsieur Lentille, the famous wild-animal photographer,
came back to his camp, he raised his arms in surprise
upon seeing a lion sprawled on his bed.
But then he cried at once:
"It's the Happy Lion! I know him.
I photographed him many times in his garden.
Quelle aventure!"

He woke up the Happy Lion after taking his picture,
and they embraced each other like old friends.

Some days later, a telegram brought joy
to the Happy Lion's home town:
"ARRIVING BY PLANE WITH THE HAPPY LION. LENTILLE."

The town prepared itself in its Sunday best
to receive the Happy Lion on his return.
Flags flew from every window, and streamers across the streets.
And all the people, with François and the band,
were at the airport when the plane came slowly to rest.

"Hurrah for the Happy Lion," everybody cried at once
while the band played the Marseillaise.
"Welcome home, Happy Lion."
And Francois could at last hug his beloved lion.

Then the Happy Lion walked back to his park
with a splendid parade to the sound of military marches.

Monsieur Lentille took many pictures
of François and the Happy Lion,
and they remained the most beautiful souvenir
of this glorious homecoming.